added copy

DATE DUE   NOV 02

FEB 13 '03			
Damage Noted Jacket Torn at Back			
GAYLORD			PRINTED IN U.S.A.

Little Tim books
by Edward Ardizzone

published by LOTHROP, LEE & SHEPARD BOOKS

Little Tim and the Brave Sea Captain
Tim to the Rescue
Tim and Charlotte
Tim in Danger
Tim and Ginger
Tim's Friend Towser

TIM TO THE RESCUE

by
Edward Ardizzone

LOTHROP, LEE & SHEPARD BOOKS
New York

First published in 1949 by Oxford University Press. Reissued in
hardcover in Great Britain by Scholastic, Ltd., 1999, and in the United States
by Lothrop, Lee & Shepard Books in 2000. Published by arrangement
with the Estate of Edward Ardizzone.

Lothrop, Lee & Shepard Books
a division of William Morrow and Company, Inc.
1350 Avenue of the Americas, New York, NY 10019

Printed in Belgium

2 3 4 5 6 7 8 9 10

Library of Congress Cataloging-in-Publication Data
Ardizzone, Edward, 1900–1979.
Tim to the rescue/by Edward Ardizzone.
p. cm.
Summary: Having gone back to sea as second ship's boy, Tim
befriends Ginger, the first ship's boy, and rescues him during a great storm.
ISBN 0-688-17679-8
[1. Sea stories.] I. Title.

PZ7.A682 Tim 2000
[E]—dc21
99-047251

Little Tim was in his house by the sea. It was stormy weather and Tim who was tired of his books and lessons was looking out of the window and was wishing that he was at sea again and having tremendous adventures on some ship tossing about among the waves.

But Tim had promised his parents to stay at home and work hard and a promise like this has to be kept.

"Oh dear," said Tim to himself, "I am bored with my sums, but I suppose I must learn them if I am to become a real grown up sailor."
Suddenly there was a
knock at the door.

It was Tim's great friend, Captain McFee, the old sea captain.

"Fine news, my boy," said McFee. "I am tired of being a landlubber so I have got a ship again. The *S.S. Fidelity* of 3000 Tons."

Tim longed more than anything else to go to sea with the captain and he begged his mother and father to let him go.

At last, as he had been a good boy and had worked hard at his lessons, they agreed, but said that he could go for one voyage only, and that he must promise to work at his lesson books in his spare time.

Captain McFee was pleased. He would take Tim as second ship's boy, but he warned Tim that once on board they could not be the same sort of friends as before. On board he was the skipper and discipline must be maintained. "Aye Aye, Sir," said Tim. Soon the great day for leaving arrived. Tim's father and mother came

to see him off. His mother cried a little when he waved goodbye. Tim could not help feeling rather sad and lonely too.

The first person Tim met on board was a tall red-haired boy called Ginger.

"Blimey," said Ginger, "What's 'ere? A blooming passenger or is it the new third mate?" This made Tim cross, but he answered politely that he was the second ship's boy.

"Second ship's boy," said Ginger. "Well, I am first ship's boy, so you will jolly well have to do what I tell you or I will bash you. I've a good mind to bash you now just to teach you."

However, as Tim did not move and did not seem afraid, Ginger became quite nice. He showed Tim the cabin they were to share and took him to see the Bosun. On the way he warned Tim to avoid the captain as he was a regular Tartar. Knowing

Captain McFee, Tim could not help feeling surprised, but perhaps people change when they go on board a ship. Would he become a Tartar, too?

The Bosun seemed quite kind and said to Tim, "Do what you are told and look slippy about it and you will be all right."

"Aye Aye," said Tim smartly.

Soon the ship started. Tim and Ginger leant on the rail and watched as they moved slowly down the wide river to the open sea.

Once at sea, Tim was kept busy doing odd jobs. But when the weather was fine and he had no duties to do, he would sit on deck in some sunny spot and study hard.

Soon he had the reputation of being a scholar.

He gave lessons in –
<u>READING & WRITING</u> to Ginger, who was very backward. <u>ARITHMETIC</u> to Fireman Jones, who wanted to become an engineer. <u>HISTORY</u> to Alaska Pete, who had a passion for King Charles I and wanted to know all about him. In the evening Tim wrote letters for Old Joe the cook, who could not read or write at all.

Ginger, I am sorry to say, was a lazy and mischievous boy. Instead of working, he would hide in some corner and look at comics. When he was hungry he would steal the seamen's marmalade, and when he wished to amuse himself he teased the ship's cat, which made Tim very cross because he liked cats. Now Ginger's worst mischief was to have the most terrible results for him.

The Third Mate was very bald and rather vain. He had in his cabin many bottles filled with different coloured hair growers.

One day Ginger went to his cabin with a message and finding he was out could not resist trying all the bottles on his head.

The last bottle that Ginger tried had a very curious shape and was full of a strange smelling green liquid.

When he put it on his head it gave him a lovely tingly feeling.

grow it

HASSAN'S MAGIC HAIR RESTORER

Guaranteed to grow Hair

Poor Ginger! Little did he know what was happening. His hair was growing and growing and GROWING.

"Crikey," said Tim
when he met
Ginger on the
deck, "Go and
get your hair
cut before
the captain
sees you."

Ginger had his hair cut, but alas to no avail. In one hour's time it was like this.

In two hours time like this, and soon it would have become like this if the captain had not seen him.

"Bosun!" roared Captain McFee, "Get that boy's hair cut."

From now on Ginger had a terrible time. Everybody who saw him shouted "Go and get your hair cut!" until he was almost in tears of dismay.

Alaska Pete and Joe the cook spent so much time making horrid mixtures to stop his hair growing (the mixtures never did)

that they neglected the cooking, which made the crew very cross.

Seaman Bloggs, the ship's barber, said that he was sick and tired of it, that his fingers were worn to the bone and that he ought to have extra pay.

In fact the ship was going to the dogs.

Ginger became so unhappy that he took to hiding in the boats. His only friends were Tim and the ship's cat, which says a lot for cats, considering how nasty Ginger had been to it.

Tim would visit Ginger as often as he could and would bring him his dinner and cut his hair with a large pair of scissors that he had borrowed from Seaman Bloggs.

And so things went on from bad to worse. One day the sky became cloudy and the sea had an oily swell. The crew grumbled about the food. The bosun was worried and the new mixture that Pete and Joe were making smelt so horribly that even the ship's cat was put off his dinner.

Tim was standing on the bridge when he heard Captain McFee say to the Mate,

"What do you think of the weather Mr Mate? I don't like it a bit. There is a hurricane blowing up or I'll eat my hat.

Order all hands on deck to batten down hatches and see that the ship's boys keep below."

The next few hours were busy ones for the crew making everything secure and shipshape on the decks. By now the wind was blowing great guns and the waves were getting bigger and bigger, occasionally

dashing over the side and wetting the crew with spray. But where was Ginger all this time? Still hiding in the boat.

Tim had tried hard to make him come below but he just would not.

In the meantime, Tim was sitting with Old Joe in the galley. He was terribly

worried about Ginger thinking how cold and hungry he must be up there in the great gale.

Finally, orders or no orders, he decided  to go to him once more and try and persuade him to come down. Tim crept up the companionway and with great difficulty pushed open the door onto the deck.

What he saw there made him very frightened. The sky was black with flying cloud, the wind was shrieking and great waves towered up on every side as if at any moment they would swamp the ship.

Standing there, the thought came to him that Ginger must be saved. He must somehow get to him and force him to come below.

Tim waited for a moment until he
thought it was a little calmer, then he
dashed across the deck; but half way there

a great wave came overboard and nearly
swept him away. He just managed to save
himself and reach the boat.

Inside the boat was Ginger. He was cold, wet and frightened and was holding the ship's cat in his arms. "Come below with me," shouted Tim again and again; but the wild wind only blew his words away.

At last Ginger heard. "No!" he cried "I can't, I am too frightened." Nothing that

Tim could do or say would make him move, so Tim left him to go back and get the crew to help. He had only gone a short way on his dangerous homeward journey when a tremendous wave rushed down upon him. He leapt for the rigging and then

looked round.
There was no boat,
no Ginger, and no cat.

Tim was horrified. "Poor Ginger, poor puss," he thought. Then in the backwash of the wave he saw the half drowned cat.

Quickly he pulled it out of the water and put it in the rigging.

Next he saw a great red mop of hair floating by. It was Ginger's. He grabbed it and hung on. He thought his arm would break, so hard did the rushing water try to tug Ginger away.

Captain McFee had seen them. "All hands to the rescue," he shouted.

Alaska Pete and Old Joe tied themselves to ropes and with tremendous courage dashed across the deck and soon had carried all three of them back to safety.

The captain seemed furious. "How dare

you disobey my orders and be on deck?"
he said to Tim and Ginger. "Go below
at once and if I catch you on deck
again I will have you both beaten with a
rope's end."

"Bosun!" he roared, "Get that boy's
HAIR CUT."

However, as they left to go Tim saw the captain brush a tear from his eye and heard him say:

"Drat those boys, Mr Mate, wouldn't lose them for the world. Fine boy, Tim. Fine boy."

Once below, Pete and Joe wrapped them in blankets and put them to bed.

Seaman Bloggs cut Ginger's hair while Joe gave them mugs of hot cocoa, and a dish of warm milk to the cat.

Alaska Pete insisted on taking their

temperatures and dosing them with some very nasty medicine to prevent them getting chills. Soon they were all asleep.

Tim woke up feeling very well. He looked at Ginger and had a great surprise. Ginger's hair had not grown at all.

"Are you well, Ginger?" Tim said. "Yes, fine," answered Ginger. "Well, look at yourself in the glass," said Tim. You can just imagine how pleased and surprised Ginger was to see his nice short hair.

Now, curious to tell, perhaps it was the cold sea water, perhaps it was the shock; but from this time on Ginger's hair grew in the ordinary slow way. In a few days time the sun came out, the sea was calm, and the weather became warm and fine.

Tim and Ginger were back at their usual jobs, the crew were busy hanging out their clothes to dry, when the captain ordered all hands to the forward well deck. There he made a speech from the bridge.

"Men," he said, "during the storm the two ship's boys disobeyed my orders and nearly got drowned.

However, now that I have heard the full story I realise that ship's boy

Tim only went on deck to rescue his
companion Ginger. It was a very gallant
action and I am going to ask the Royal

Humane Society to give him a gold medal."
– Cheers from the crew – "Alaska Pete and
Old Joe," the Captain continued, "were

very brave to face the raging sea and rescue the two boys and the cat. I will give them each £5" – loud cheers – "But I hope that in the future they will both give up making nasty smelling mixtures and get on with the cooking" – prolonged cheers. As you can imagine after this Tim was very popular with everyone.

Ginger was a reformed character. He worked well and became quite popular too.

Joe and Pete were their special friends. In the evening when the day's work was done, they would sit together and tell stories. Tim thrilled them all with tales of how he was shipwrecked and of Mr Grimes and the mutineers. Joe was so impressed that he always called Tim the little skipper.

From now on too the Bosun took a special interest in Tim and spent much time teaching him many things that a sailor should know. Tim would repeat the lessons to Ginger who became quite clever.

But with all this you must not think that Tim neglected his lesson books, because he did not.

After a long and happy voyage the ship came back to port. Tim's mother and father were on the dock to meet him. They invited Ginger to stay with them which he was very pleased to do, as he had no home of his own.

Tim went back to school and Ginger went with him. Tim was first in class for Reading, Writing, Arithmetic, History and Geography, which just goes to show how hard he had worked at his books.

Ginger was second in Geography, which showed that he had worked hard too.

But Tim's proudest moment came when there arrived by post a beautiful gold medal and a roll of parchment on which was written the story of his brave adventure. Tim's father had the roll framed and hung it in the drawing room.

— THE END —